BEN MANLEY ❦ EMMA CHICHESTER CLARK

Constance
— IN —
PERIL

TWO HOOTS

For Florence and Robin – BM

First published 2021 by Two Hoots
an imprint of Pan Macmillan

The Smithson
6 Briset Street
London
EC1M 5NR

EU representative:
Macmillan Publishers Ireland Limited
Mallard Lodge, Lansdowne Village, Dublin 4

Associated companies throughout the world
www.panmacmillan.com
ISBN 978-1-5098-3973-5

Text copyright © Ben Manley 2021
Illustrations copyright © Emma Chichester Clark 2021
Moral rights asserted.

1 3 5 7 9 8 6 4 2

A CIP catalogue record for this book is available from the British Library.

Printed in China

The illustrations in this book were created using gouache.
With thanks to Suzanne Carnell, Chris Inns, Sharon King-Chai, Tony Fleetwood and Jenny Shone

www.twohootsbooks.com

FSC
www.fsc.org

MIX
Paper from
responsible sources
FSC® C116313

EDWARD'S favourite toy was a soft, old, cloth doll.
Her name was Constance Hardpenny
and she had led a tragic life.

Edward didn't know where she had come from,
but he took her to his heart and gave her a home.

There she lived
happily for a time.

But Constance was no
stranger to misfortune and
disaster was never far behind.

On Monday,

Constance became
trapped at the top of
the hornbeam tree
with no chance
of rescue.

Until . . .

On Tuesday,

Constance tarried too
long in the howling rain
and was sure to catch
her death.

Until . . .

On Wednesday,

Constance lodged herself
between the iron railings
in the playground and
almost lost an arm.

Until . . .

On Thursday,

Constance fell into the jaws
of the neighbour's spaniel
and was certain to perish.

Until . . .

On Friday,

Constance was kidnapped by a
gang of notorious ruffians and
held to a king's ransom.

Until . . .

But the worst was yet to
come for poor, unfortunate
Constance Hardpenny.

On Saturday,

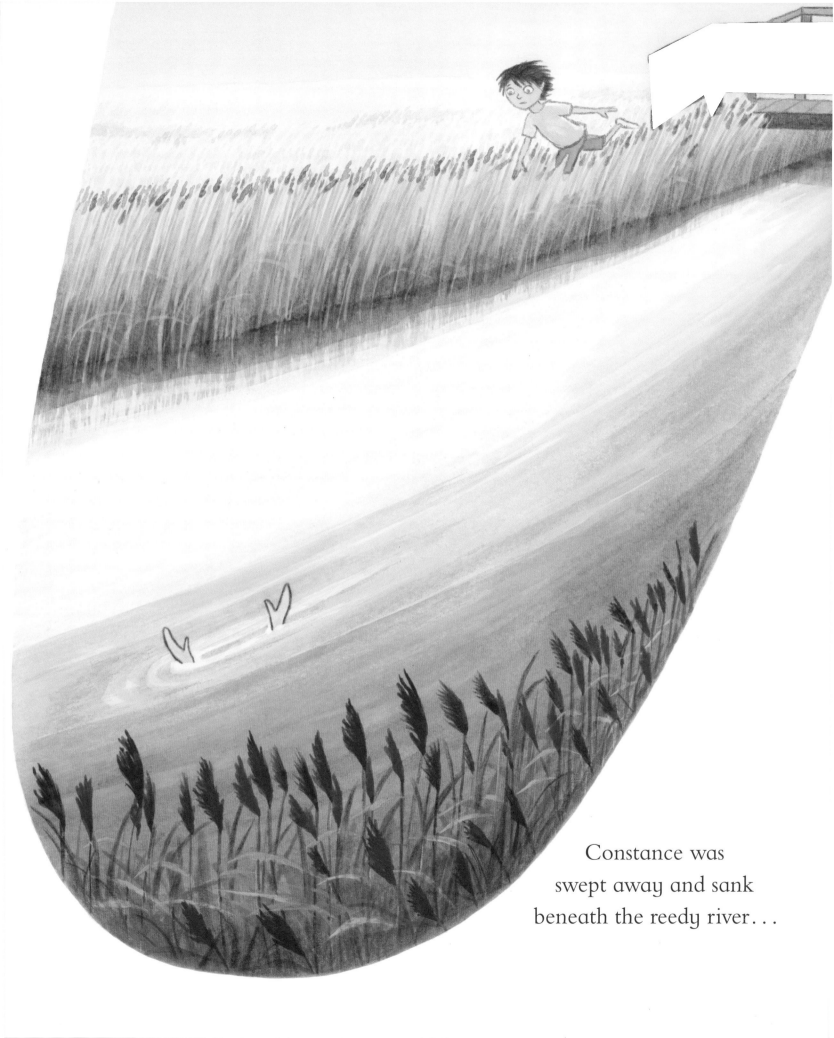

Constance was
swept away and sank
beneath the reedy river...

. . . forever.

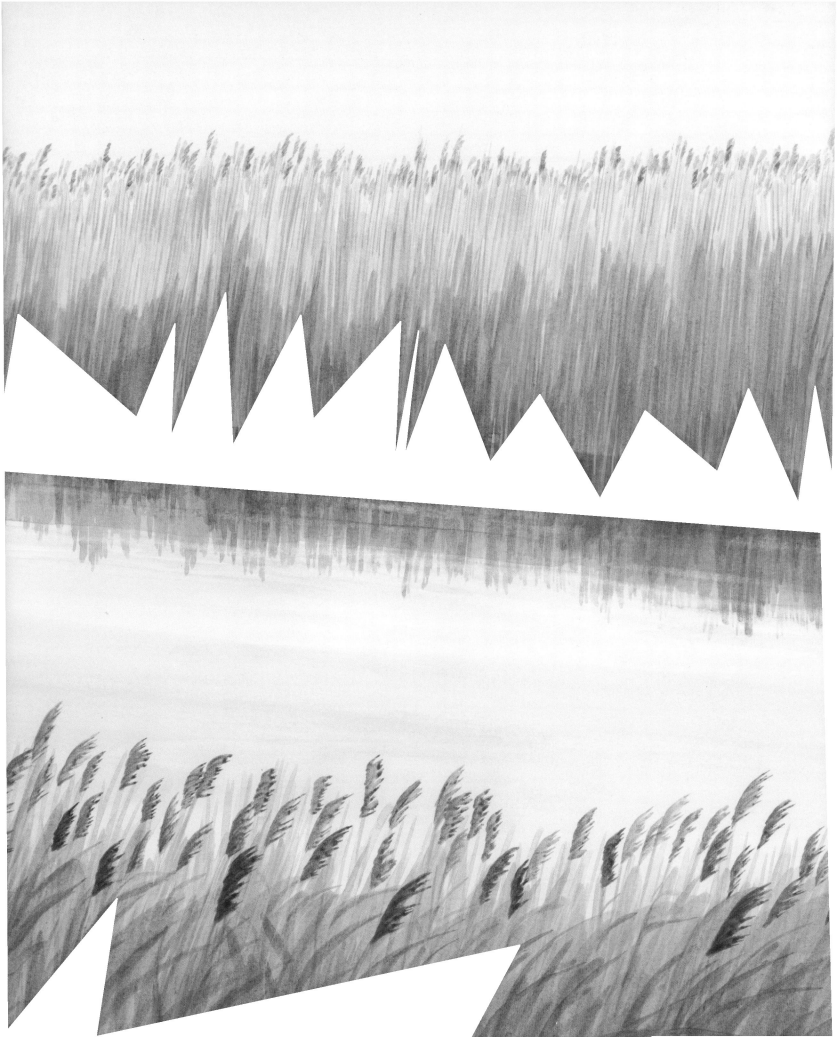

Until . . .

On Sunday,

after suffering much
misfortune and surviving
fathomless perils . . .

Constance lived happily ever after.